Rana Pratap

RAJASTHAN IN WESTERN INDIA WAS THE HOME OF THE VALIANT RAJPUTS.

THROUGHOUT HISTORY, THEY HAD REPEATEDLY FOUGHT FOR THE HONOUR OF THE COUNTRY.

BUT THE RAJPUTS OF CHITTOR SURPASSED ALL, IN DEEDS OF BRAVERY AND PERSONAL SACRIFICE.

IN THE EIGHTH CENTURY A.D. THEY REPULSED AN INVASION OF THEIR LAND.

AND THEIR WOMEN WERE NO LESS HEROIC. CHITTOR'S QUEEN KARMA DEVI HAD DEFEATED THE POWERFUL HORDES OF QUTAB-UD-DIN.

IN THE 14TH CENTURY, QUEEN PADMINI AND HUNDREDS OF RAJPUT WOMEN OF CHITTOR PERFORMED SATI, AN ACT OF SELF-IMMOLATION TO SAVE THEIR HONOUR FROM THE INVADER, ALA-UD-DIN KHILJI.

THE MUGHALS WERE THE FIRST INVADERS WHO SUCCEEDED IN OCCUPYING CHITTOR.

ALMOST ALL MAJOR RAJPUT KINGS HAD SURRENDERED TO THE ENEMY BUT RANA PRATAP, THE KING OF CHITTOR, REFUSED TO.

I SWEAR THAT I WILL SACRIFICE MY VERY LIFE FOR CHITTOR.

WE ALSO PLEDGE THAT TILL WE ATTAIN FREEDOM, WE WILL NOT SLEEP ON A BED BUT ON THE GROUND AND WE WILL NOT WEAR FANCY CLOTHES.

MAY GODDESS KALI BLESS YOU RANAJI, YOU HAVE TAKEN A TERRIBLE OATH.

GURUDEV, DEFENDING ONE'S MOTHERLAND IS A SERIOUS MATTER...

... AND NO SACRIFICE IS TOO BIG FOR SUCH A NOBLE CAUSE.

WE WILL FIGHT FOR FREEDOM WITH THE LAST DROP OF OUR BLOOD.

WELL SAID. BUT OUR TASK IS A DIFFICULT ONE. MANY OF OUR OWN PEOPLE ARE HELPING THE INVADERS.

WE MUST INCREASE OUR STRENGTH. LET'S CAPTURE AN IMPORTANT FORT FIRST.

SO, A HANDFUL OF RANA PRATAP'S WARRIORS ATTACKED A FORT, UNDER MUGHAL OCCUPATION, NEAR CHITTOR.

HAR HAR MAHADEV!

JAI CHANDI!

FINALLY THE MUGHAL FORCES WERE DEFEATED.

WELL DONE, MY MEN! THE FORT IS OURS.

THIS VICTORY BROUGHT MANY RAJPUTS FROM CHITTOR TO THE FORT TO JOIN PRATAP'S FORCES.

TELL THE PEOPLE OF CHITTOR THAT THOUGH THEY ARE RULED BY THE INVADERS...

...I AM THEIR TRUE KING. I ORDER THAT NOBODY SHALL TILL THE LAND TILL WE ATTAIN FREEDOM.

MEANWHILE, IN THE COURT OF AKBAR —

HAVE YOU HEARD THE LATEST JOKE? PRATAP STILL CALLS HIMSELF THE KING OF CHITTOR.

OF COURSE, HE IS A KING BUT WITHOUT A KINGDOM.

SILENCE! YOU FORGET THAT PRATAP HAS TAKEN A FORT.

BUT SIR, OUR HUGE ARMY CAN CRUSH HIM IN NO TIME.

YOU ARE WRONG. IT IS NOT GOING TO BE EASY TO CRUSH PRATAP.

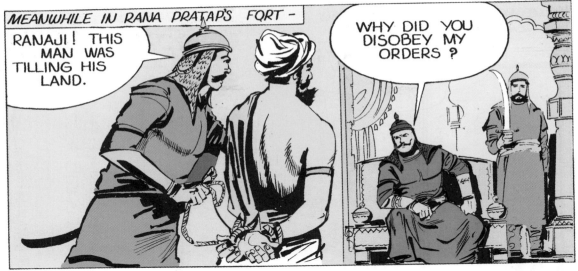

MEANWHILE IN RANA PRATAP'S FORT —

RANAJI! THIS MAN WAS TILLING HIS LAND.

WHY DID YOU DISOBEY MY ORDERS?

BUT I HAD TAKEN THE PERMISSION OF THE MUGHAL GOVERNOR.

I AM THE KING OF CHITTOR AND I HAVE NOT GIVEN YOU THE PERMISSION...

...YOUR CROP WILL FINALLY FEED THE ENEMY AND THUS HELP HIM.

FOR ACTING AGAINST THE INTEREST OF OUR MOTHER-LAND, YOU SHALL DIE!

THE FOLLOWING DAY, THE FARMER WAS HANGED.

THE NEWS OF THE FARMER'S DEATH REACHED AKBAR.

THIS IS OUTRAGEOUS. PERHAPS HE CAN STILL BE WON OVER.

AKBAR CONSULTED HIS RAJPUT COMMANDER, MAN SINGH.

A BRAVE MAN LIKE PRATAP SHOULD BE OUR FRIEND, RAJA MAN SINGH. PLEASE GO AND ASK HIM TO STOP THIS REVOLT AGAINST US.

YOU ARE RIGHT, SIR. HIS FRIENDSHIP CAN BE AN ASSET TO THE MUGHAL EMPIRE.

AND SO MAN SINGH WENT TO MEET RANA PRATAP. HE WAS RECEIVED BY PRATAP'S MINISTER.

WELCOME, SIR, MAN SINGH!

I HAVE A MESSAGE. MAHARAJ AKBAR, THE KING OF BHARAT, SEEKS RANAJI'S FRIENDSHIP.

HE MAY BE A KING FOR YOU, BUT TO US HE IS AN INVADER, AN ENEMY.

IT IS TREASON TO RISE AGAINST THE KING.

IT IS NOT TREASON BUT OUR SACRED DUTY TO FIGHT FOR OUR FREEDOM.

BUT WHY DON'T YOU REALISE THAT YOU CAN'T DEFEAT OUR HUGE FORCES.

WE SHALL DO OUR DUTY WHETHER WE WIN OR NOT.

RANA PRATAP ENTERED WITH HIS SON, AMAR SINGH.

THAT IS ENOUGH FOR NOW, MINISTER WE WILL DISCUSS THE MATTER LATER. RAJA MAN SINGH MUST BE HUNGRY. LET US OFFER HIM OUR SIMPLE FOOD, AMAR.

YES FATHER!

WON'T YOU JOIN ME?

NO, YOU ARE OUR GUEST. SO, YOU MUST EAT BEFORE US.

BUT THE HOST MUST ALSO EAT WITH THE GUEST.

I AM SORRY, BUT I CAN'T EAT WITH YOU.

MAY I KNOW WHY?

SOON AFTER MAN SINGH LEFT, RANA PRATAP ATTACKED A CAMP OF MUGHAL FORCES AND KILLED MANY OF THEM.

IN THE COURT OF AKBAR—

PRATAP HAS LEFT US NO OTHER ALTERNATIVE. WE WILL HAVE TO CRUSH HIM.

VERY WELL, THEN DO IT.

SOON MAN SINGH AND PRINCE SALIM SET OUT WITH A HUGE ARMY.

IF WE CAN DRIVE PRATAP OUT OF HIS FORT, THEN OUR TASK WILL BECOME EASY.

YES, WITH OUR LARGE ARMY WE CAN DEFEAT HIM.

FINALLY AKBAR'S FORCES REACHED THE FAMOUS BATTLE-GROUND, HALDI-GHATI, SITUATED IN A NARROW VALLEY.

NOW BEGINS THE TOUGHEST PART OF OUR JOB.

MAN SINGH ALSO RECEIVED VITAL INFORMATION.

COMMANDER MAN SINGH, PRATAP HAS ONLY 22,000 SOLDIERS AND THEY HAVE NO GUNS.

THAT IS GOOD NEWS.

THIS MAN PRATAP MUST BE STUPID TO CHALLENGE THE MUGHAL EMPIRE WITHOUT ENOUGH SOLDIERS AND GOOD WEAPONS.

BRAVE, NOT STUPID! HE IS A TRUE RAJPUT AND...

...DON'T BE OVERCONFIDENT, PRINCE. HUGE ARMIES AND GOOD WEAPONS DO HELP IN A BATTLE. BUT WHEN IT COMES TO FIGHTING, THERE IS NO SUBSTITUTE FOR COURAGE.

LET US STOP THIS IDLE CHATTER AND ATTACK.

WE CAN'T.

WHY NOT?

BECAUSE THE WAY TO PRATAP'S FORT LIES THROUGH THAT NARROW VALLEY AND...

...PRATAP'S SOLDIERS ARE WAITING THERE TO TRAP US. WE WILL HAVE TO WAIT FOR THEM TO ATTACK FIRST.

AFTER A LONG WAIT —

WE CAN'T WAIT INDEFINITELY. LET US ATTACK AT ONCE.

NO, PRINCE SALIM!

SIR, I HAVE FOUND A LONG BUT EASY PATH LEADING TO PRATAP'S FORT.

GOOD, TAKE ENOUGH SOLDIERS AND ATTACK THE FORT FROM THE REAR.

YES SIR!

AND A STRONG MUGHAL FORCE MARCHED OFF TO SURROUND RANA PRATAP'S FORT.

WHEN RANA PRATAP HEARD ABOUT THIS NEW TROOP MOVEMENT, HE WAS WORRIED.

THE BEST STRATEGY WOULD HAVE BEEN TO FIGHT FROM THE FORT BUT NOW WE HAVE TO FACE THEM IN HALDI-GHATI.

FINALLY IN THE VALLEY CALLED HALDI-GHATI —

ATTACK!

PRATAP AND HIS SOLDIERS CHARGED FIERCELY.

EVEN PRATAP'S FAITHFUL HORSE CHETAK PARTICIPATED IN THE BATTLE.

THE MUGHAL FORCES SUFFERED HEAVY LOSSES.

BUT JUST WHEN THE MUGHALS STARTED TO LOSE, MORE OF THEIR TROOPS ARRIVED.

IN THE BITTER FIGHTING THAT FOLLOWED, RANA PRATAP LOST 15,000 MEN.

BUT THE BATTLE CONTINUED.

MAN SINGH IS AN ABLE COMMANDER. IF HE IS KILLED, HIS FORCES WILL LOSE THEIR MORALE.

RANA PRATAP ADVANCED TOWARDS MAN SINGH.

MAN SINGH WAS RIDING AN ELEPHANT. PRATAP ATTACKED HIM LIKE A FIERCE LION.

PRATAP THREW HIS SPEAR AT MAN SINGH, BUT JUST THEN THE ELEPHANT MOVED AND PRATAP MISSED HIS MARK. MAN SINGH WAS SAVED.

MEANWHILE PRATAP WAS SURROUNDED BY ENEMY SOLDIERS.

FINDING THEIR LEADER IN DANGER, PRATAP'S FRIEND, MANA AND A FEW SOLDIERS RUSHED TO HIS RESCUE.

OUR RANA IS WOUNDED. I MUST SAVE HIM.

TO SAVE PRATAP, MANA PLACED PRATAP'S HELMET ON HIS OWN HEAD.

THE MUGHAL SOLDIERS WERE FOOLED. THEY ATTACKED MANA, MISTAKING HIM FOR PRATAP. WHILE MANA FACED THE ENEMY, PRATAP WAS CARRIED AWAY BY HIS FAITHFUL HORSE, CHETAK.

SOME RAJPUT SOLDIERS RODE WITH CHETAK TO PROTECT THE UNCONSCIOUS RANA.

THE WOUNDED PRATAP WAS TAKEN TO A CAVE IN THE JUNGLES.

THOUGH PRATAP SURVIVED, HIS FAMILY HAD A HARD TIME. FOR SEVERAL DAYS THEY HAD NOTHING TO EAT BUT WILD BERRIES AND ROOTS.

ONE DAY, WHEN PRATAP'S SON, AMAR SINGH, WAS EATING A DRY CHAPATI...

FATHER, THE CAT SNATCHED MY CHAPATI.

PRATAP'S DAUGHTER, WHO GAVE HER CHAPATI TO HER BROTHER, FAINTED DUE TO HUNGER.

I CAN'T BEAR IT ANY MORE. I SHALL WRITE TO AKBAR.

SOME TIME LATER, IN AKBAR'S COURT —

AT LAST RANA PRATAP HAS DECIDED TO BOW DOWN TO ME. THIS IS AN OCCASION FOR CELEBRATION.

PRITHVIRAJ, A RAJPUT POET IN AKBAR'S COURT, WAS A SECRET ADMIRER OF PRATAP. HE DID NOT LIKE THE NEWS.

SO THE LAST HOPE OF FREEDOM IS ALSO LOST. I MUST DO SOMETHING ABOUT IT.

AND POET PRITHVIRAJ SENT A LETTER TO RANA PRATAP.

You alone can preserve the honour of the Rajputs. The sun would sooner rise in the west than have you address Akbar as your Lord.

INSPIRING WORDS! I MUST WRITE TO HIM THAT THE SUN WILL CONTINUE TO RISE IN THE EAST. I WILL NEVER BOW BEFORE AKBAR.

UNAWARE OF PRITHVIRAJ'S LETTER, AKBAR SENT A LARGE BAND OF SOLDIERS TO ESCORT PRATAP FROM THE JUNGLES.

WHEN RANA PRATAP REFUSED TO GO WITH THEM, THE SOLDIERS ATTACKED HIM.

WE ARE GREATLY OUTNUMBERED.

FIGHT, MY BRAVE MEN!

SOON ALL THE RAJPUT SOLDIERS WERE KILLED AND PRATAP WAS ABOUT TO BE CAPTURED, WHEN A BAND OF BHIL TRIBALS ATTACKED THE MUGHALS.

THE BHILS RESCUED PRATAP AND HIS FAMILY AND CARRIED THEM TO THEIR VILLAGE. PRATAP WAS SAD OVER THE LOSS OF HIS SOLDIERS.

EVERYTHING IS FINISHED NOW. I CAN'T LIBERATE MY MOTHERLAND.

YOU SHOULDN'T LOSE HEART, RANAJI. YOU ARE OUR ONLY HOPE.

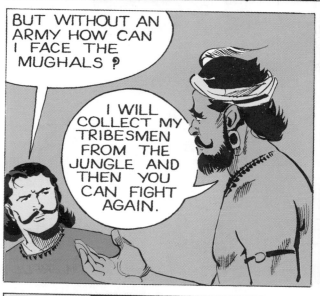

BUT WITHOUT AN ARMY HOW CAN I FACE THE MUGHALS?

I WILL COLLECT MY TRIBESMEN FROM THE JUNGLE AND THEN YOU CAN FIGHT AGAIN.

BUT FOR RAISING AN ARMY WE NEED MONEY AND I HAVE NONE.

ONE DAY—

I CAN'T REMAIN A BURDEN ON YOU ANY MORE. I SHALL GO AWAY FROM HERE.

YOU ARE NOT A BURDEN, RANAJI.

JUST THEN A MESSENGER ARRIVED.

RANAJI, A PERSON CALLED BHAMA SHAH WANTS TO MEET YOU.

BRING HIM IN.

RANAJI, I HEARD THAT YOU NEED MONEY. MY WEALTH IS AT YOUR DISPOSAL.

BUT I CAN'T ACCEPT YOUR PERSONAL PROPERTY.

BHAMA SHAH WAS A PROMINENT BUSINESSMAN OF CHITTOR.

NOTHING REMAINS PERSONAL WHEN OUR COUNTRY IS IN TROUBLE. NOW EVERY-THING BELONGS TO THE COUNTRY.

WITH THE HELP OF THIS HUGE WEALTH, PRATAP RAISED A POWERFUL ARMY OF BHILS.

NOW, WE ARE PREPARED TO FIGHT THE MUGHALS AGAIN.

JAI CHANDI! HAR HAR MAHADEV!

PRATAP LED THE BRAVE BHILS TO MANY VICTORIES.

THE FORT OF PHINSAHRA WAS WON FROM THE MUGHALS.

THEN PRATAP SWIFTLY ATTACKED OTHER NEARBY FORTS UNDER MUGHAL OCCUPATION.

FINALLY RANA PRATAP MANAGED TO LIBERATE THE AREAS OF DEVAR, UDAIPUR AND KOMALMIR.

BUT CHITTOR WAS STILL OCCUPIED BY THE MUGHALS. PRATAP HAD FOUGHT RELENTLESSLY FOR TWENTY YEARS. NOW HE WAS VERY SICK.

SOON YOU WOULD BE HEALTHY AGAIN, RANAJI!

NO, I KNOW THAT MY END HAS COME.

HOW UNLUCKY I AM THAT I COULD NOT LIBERATE MY MOTHER-LAND, CHITTOR.

THUS WITH HIS DREAM ONLY PARTIALLY FULFILLED, RANA PRATAP PASSED AWAY. TILL THE LAST DAY OF HIS LIFE, HE STRICTLY ADHERED TO HIS OATH. EVEN WHEN HE WAS SICK, HE DID NOT SLEEP ON A COMFORTABLE BED, BUT ON THE GROUND. THUS RANA PRATAP SET AN EXAMPLE TO LEADERS OF ALL TIMES THAT THEY HAD NO RIGHT TO LIVE IN LUXURY WHEN THE COUNTRY SUFFERED.